22803

22803

THE
NUTCRACKER
BALLET

VLADIMIR VAGIN

SCHOLASTIC
HARDCOVER

SCHOLASTIC INC.

NEW YORK

SCHOLASTIC HARDCOVER is a registered trademark of Scholastic Inc.,
555 Broadway, New York, NY 10012.
Cataloging-in-Publication Data available
Library of Congress number: 94-30716
ISBN 0-590-47220-8
CIP
AC
12 11 10 9 8 7 6 5 4 3 2 1   5 6 7 8 9/9 0/0
Printed in the United States of America   37
First printing, October 1995
Mr. Vagin's pictures were drawn first in pencil
and then painted in watercolor.
Production supervision by Angela Biola
Designed by Vladimir Vagin

For the enchanting girl, Emma,
and the two lovely sisters,
Lucy and Ava

It was Christmas Eve, a night for magic. Anything could happen. Clara and her brother Fritz waited outside the door to the parlor. Their cousins crowded around. Would they catch a glimpse of the presents? Of the tree?

The children spilled into the parlor. The tree, full and fragrant, rose grandly before them. Sweets hung from its branches. Candles lit its boughs.

Clara's cheeks flushed with excitement. She ran to greet her godfather, Herr Drosselmeier. He was an inventor and always brought the most unusual gifts, toys unlike any the children had seen.

This year, Herr Drosselmeier arrived bearing three tall boxes, each wrapped in festive paper and tied with bright ribbon. He opened the first.

In the box was a soldier, outfitted in full, regimental dress. When the soldier was wound, he saluted smartly and clicked his heels.

Harlequin and Columbine stepped out of the next boxes. The two clowns tumbled into somersaults, then dove into handsprings. They topped it all with a sprightly jig.

Finally, Clara's godfather brought out a small, wooden soldier, no bigger than a doll. The soldier's hair was snow-white. His head was large and his features coarse. Herr Drosselmeier placed a nut in the strange soldier's mouth. *Crack!* The soldier was a nutcracker! Herr Drosselmeier handed Clara the Nutcracker and sweet nutmeat.

Before Clara could taste the treat, Fritz bounded up and grabbed the Nutcracker from her. He jammed a nut in its mouth. *Snap!* With one careless tug, Fritz broke the Nutcracker's jaw.

The children's father grabbed Fritz by the collar and scolded him roundly. Herr Drosselmeier shook out a handkerchief and wrapped the poor soldier's jaw, repairing the damage as best he could.

That night, after the party, when the others had long since retired to bed, Clara crept back to the parlor and cradled the wounded soldier in her arms. The hour drifted toward midnight. As Clara sunk sleepily onto the sofa, Herr Drosselmeier stepped from the shadows. He eased the Nutcracker from the little girl's grasp. With a turn here and a twist there, he mended the soldier's jaw.

Bong! The clock struck twelve. Clara started. Was that Herr Drosselmeier on top of the grandfather clock? And what was that scampering sound? Clara hid behind the safety of the sofa.

A mouse scurried across the room, brandishing a sharp saber. Clara gasped. The mouse was as large as she! The Christmas tree, too, began to grow — and grow and grow — until the top branch of the tree scraped the ceiling. Fritz's toy soldiers, spirited and tall, marched out in tight formation. Even the Nutcracker had grown as large as Clara!

Just then, an army of mice charged across the room, attacking the toys. They were led by the Mouse King, a leering, frightful creature with seven heads. The toy soldiers fought valiantly, but they were vastly outnumbered. The Mouse King pinned the Nutcracker with his sword.

"No!" cried Clara. She hurled her slipper at the Mouse King, knocking him flat. The Nutcracker leaped to his feet. He thrust his sword through the Mouse King's heart. The toys were the victors! He lifted the crown from the Mouse King's head and placed it atop Clara's.

As the Nutcracker crowned Clara, the walls of the parlor dissolved into the night. Clara found herself standing at the foot of a snowswept hill. White stars glistened in the blue-black sky. Snowflakes fell as softly as blossoms.

Before Clara's eyes, the Nutcracker shed his awkward wooden figure and turned into a handsome prince! He tossed back his cape and bowed deeply before her. Clara glanced down. She was now dressed in a gown of rich brocade, the gown of a princess! Was this a dream or enchantment? The Prince took Clara by the hand. He led her to the edge of the ice-bright shore.

Clara and the Prince stepped aboard a boat with a graceful, billowing sail. The boat floated up a river of nectar and honey. It passed trees hung with peppermint drops and arrived at a palace studded with glazed, sugary spires. "My home is the Land of Sweets," explained the Prince. "I rule from the Marzipan Castle."

At the gates of the castle, Clara and the Prince were met by the Sugar Plum Fairy and the delicate angels who attended her. "Welcome home," the Fairy greeted the Prince. Then the Prince told the tale of his battle with the Mouse King and introduced his friend. "Clara was brave in battle," he said. "She struck down the Mouse King and saved my life."

With great ceremony, Clara and the Prince were
led to the banquet hall, where they took their places
at a grand throne, set with trays of sweets. The
Sugar Plum Fairy beckoned her troupe of Delicacies.
"Let the celebration begin!" she proclaimed.

First to perform were two Hot Chocolates. They
danced a Spanish fandango, a-click with castanets.

Next came Arabian Coffee. She wore gauzy, flowing silks that shimmered as she swayed. She whirled amid a swirl of scarves, a clack and clang of bangles.

The Chinese Tea Dancers fluttered their fans. High-stepping Russians kicked up their heels, crisp as candy canes.

Mother Ginger rustled in next, wearing an enormous hoop skirt. When she parted her petticoats, children tumbled out! Six, seven, eight, and more!

Then came the Flowers, ablaze with color. Their petals were sugared in bright garden hues. Orchid pink and marigold yellow. Poppy red and wisteria blue.

The Flowers were touched by a drop of dew. As each was watered, it sprang to its toes and joined the others. Together they danced the "Waltz of the Flowers."

Finally, the Sugar Plum Fairy came to the floor, escorted by her gallant Cavalier. The two performed an elegant *pas de deux*, a fitting finale to all the dances of the candy kingdom.

As the music faded, Clara knew it was time to return home. The Delicacies bid her good-bye. Last to step forward was the Nutcracker Prince. Clara did not want to leave her friend. "I'll never be far away," the Prince reassured her. He promised Clara that they would see each other again one day.

On Christmas morning, Clara awoke snug and warm in her own bed. She recalled the adventures of the night before: the battle with the Mouse King and the journey to the Land of Sweets. Through it all, she'd had the company of her Prince. . . .

Clara hugged the Nutcracker to her. She wanted no other present. For Clara now knew a secret of Christmas—that magic is the best present of all.